Puffin Books

UNstoppaBLE!

What the experts say about Paul Jennings:

'When I read your books I laugh until my head rolls off.' **Claire,** *Warwickshire, UK*

'Ever since I read my first Paul Jennings book, I have been addicted to them.' **Andy,** *Leicestershire, UK*

'When my teacher reads your stories to my class, sometimes she's laughing so hard she can't finish the sentence. And for my teacher to laugh you're real magical.' **Cristina,** *New York*

'Your books are so great even football has taken a back seat. You can't imagine how hard it is to get the boys away from football.' **Danielle,** *London*

'You are a weird, wacky, wonderful, ~~funny,~~ no, make that hilarious writer.' **Shannon,** *New Plymouth, New Zealand*

'You are a cool and mad writer.' **Zoe,** *Leeming, Western Australia*

PAUL JENNINGS

Unstoppable!

Mad mad stories

PUFFIN BOOKS

PUFFIN BOOKS

Published by the Penguin Group
Penguin Books Ltd, 27 Wrights Lane, London W8 5TZ, England
Penguin Books USA Inc., 375 Hudson Street, New York, New York 10014, USA
Penguin Books Australia Ltd, Ringwood, Victoria, Australia
Penguin Books Canada Ltd, 10 Alcorn Avenue, Toronto, Ontario, Canada M4V 3B2
Penguin Books (NZ) Ltd, 182–190 Wairau Road, Auckland 10, New Zealand

Penguin Books Ltd, Registered Offices: Harmondsworth, Middlesex, England

First published 1997
1 3 5 7 9 10 8 6 4 2

'Wunderpants' and 'Lucky Lips' were first published in *Unreal!* in Australia by Penguin
Books Australia Ltd 1985, published in Great Britain in Puffin Books 1992,
copyright © Paul Jennings, 1985
'Ringing Wet' was first published in *Uncovered!* in Australia by Penguin Books Australia
Ltd 1995, published in Great Britain in Puffin Books 1996,
copyright © Paul Jennings, 1995
'Licked' was first published in *Unbearable!* in Australia by Penguin Books Australia Ltd
1991, published in Great Britain in Puffin Books 1992,
copyright © Paul Jennings, 1991

Illustrations copyright © Keith McEwan
All rights reserved

Made and printed in England by Clays Ltd, St Ives plc

CONTENTS

REMEMBER by Paul Jennings

Photograph by Martin Saller

Recently I visited the Black Country Historical Museum. They had a classroom all set up just like school used to be when I was a boy. Chalk and slates. Inkwells. Wooden desks with lift-up lids.

And a teacher. 'Sit down visitors,' she said in a firm voice.

I sat down in one of the desks with the others. Why did I do it? I was a man. I didn't have to be a kid again. But I did what I was told.

The teacher started tapping on the blackboard with a pointer and all the adults started chanting. 'Once eight is eight. Two eights are sixteen. Three eights are . . .'

I can tell you that the hair started to stand up on the back of my neck. I felt like I was really back in school. I was nervous. The teacher looked straight at me. 'Nine eights?' she barked.

Oh shoot. I never could do the eight times table. Nine eights, nine eights? What in the heck are nine eights? I couldn't think. My mind froze. 'Too slow,' she said. 'Stay in after school.'

Next we were all made to stand up and hold out our hands with the palms facing downwards. What was this for? Then I remembered back to when I was nine years old. SHE WAS INSPECTING OUR NAILS. Looking for dirty fingernails. I once had a teacher who used to whack my fingers with a ruler if she found dirt. I started to sweat.

1

Finally the teacher reached me. My nails were clean. 'Are you chewing?' she barked.

I nodded. I had just bought some bull's-eyes in the historical sweet shop. The teacher held out her hand. SHE WANTED ME TO SPIT OUT MY BULL'S-EYE. I closed my mouth and shook my head. Then I ran for the door. 'Who said you can leave the room?' she yelled. 'Where are you going?'

'I'm out of here,' I said. 'I'm off.'

Outside I stood in the fresh air and calmed down. That classroom had stirred up my memories. Being bossed around. Being a kid.

I remember as if it were yesterday.

Especially when I write.

A boy once wrote to me and said, 'Dear Paul Jennings, How come you know what it is like to be me?'

Well, I don't really know what it is like to be him. But I do remember what it is like to be a kid. When I write, I am always the boy or girl in the story. In this collection I get to be a bully who steals kisses using magic lipstick, a poor kid with weird underpants, a girl who wets the bed and loves it, and a boy who teaches his father some table manners.

And I can tell you this – no one whacks the fingers of the kids in my stories and gets away with it. Not on your life.

When you read these stories you will become the main character in each story. Some tough things will happen. You may never be the same again. But I'm not going to let anything really bad happen to you.

Am I?

Paul Jennings

WUNDERPANTS

My Dad is not a bad sort of bloke. There are plenty who are much worse. But he does rave on a bit, like if you get muddy when you are catching frogs, or rip your pants when you are building a tree hut. Stuff like that.

Mostly we understand each other and I can handle him. What he doesn't know doesn't hurt him. If he knew that I kept Snot, my pet rabbit, under the bed, he wouldn't like it; so I don't tell him. That way he is happy, I am happy and Snot is happy.

There are only problems when he finds out what has been going on. Like the time that I wanted to see *Mad Max II*. The old man said it was a bad movie – too much blood and guts.

'It's too violent,' he said.

'But, Dad, that's not fair. All the other kids are going. I'll be the only one in the school who hasn't seen it.' I went on and on like this. I kept nagging. In the end he gave in – he wasn't a bad old boy. He usually let me have what I wanted after a while. It was easy to get around him.

The trouble started the next morning. He was cleaning his teeth in the bathroom, making noises, humming and gurgling – you know the sort of thing. Suddenly he stopped. Everything went quiet. Then he came into the kitchen. There was toothpaste all around his mouth; he looked like a mad tiger. He was frothing at the mouth.

'What's this?' he said. He was waving his toothbrush about. 'What's this on my toothbrush?' Little grey hairs were sticking out of it. 'How did these hairs get on my toothbrush? Did you have my toothbrush, David?'

He was starting to get mad. I didn't know whether to own up or not. Parents always tell you that if you own up they will let you off. They say that they won't do anything if you are honest – no punishment.

I decided to give it a try. 'Yes,' I said. 'I used it yesterday.'

He still had toothpaste on his mouth. He couldn't talk properly. 'What are these little grey hairs?' he asked.

'I used it to brush my pet mouse,' I answered.

'Your what?' he screamed.

'My mouse.'

He started jumping up and down and screaming. He ran around in circles holding his throat, then he ran into the bathroom and started washing his mouth out. There was a lot of splashing and gurgling. He was acting like a madman.

I didn't know what all the fuss was about. All that yelling just over a few mouse hairs.

After a while he came back into the kitchen. He kept opening and shutting his mouth as if he could taste something bad. He had a mean look in his eye – real mean.

'What are you thinking of?' he yelled at the top of his voice. 'Are you crazy or something? Are you trying to kill me? Don't you know that mice carry germs? They are filthy things. I'll probably die of some terrible disease.'

He went on and on like this for ages. Then he said, 'And don't think that you are going to see *Mad Max II*. You can sit at home and think how stupid it is to brush a mouse with someone else's toothbrush.'

2

I went back to my room to get dressed. Dad just didn't understand about that mouse. It was a special mouse, a very special mouse indeed. It was going to make me a lot of money: fifty dollars, in fact. Every year there was a mouse race in Smith's barn. The prize was fifty dollars. And my mouse, Swift Sam, had a good chance of winning. But I had to look after him. That's why I brushed him with a toothbrush.

I knew that Swift Sam could beat every other mouse except one. There was one mouse I wasn't sure about. It was called Mugger and it was owned by Scrag Murphy, the toughest kid in the town. I had never seen his mouse, but I knew it was fast. Scrag Murphy fed it on a special diet.

That is what I was thinking about as I dressed. I went over to the cupboard to get a pair of underpants. There were none there. 'Hey, Mum,' I yelled out. 'I am out of underpants.'

Mum came into the room holding something terrible. Horrible. It was a pair of home made underpants. 'I made these for you, David,' she said. 'I bought the material at the Op Shop. There was just the right amount of material for one pair of underpants.'

'I'm not wearing those,' I told her. 'No way. Never.'

'What's wrong with them?' said Mum. She sounded hurt.

'They're pink,' I said. 'And they've got little pictures of fairies on them. I couldn't wear them. Everyone would laugh. I would be the laughing stock of the school.'

Underpants with fairies on them and pink. I nearly freaked out. I thought about what Scrag Murphy would say if he ever heard about them. I went red just thinking about it.

Just then Dad poked his head into the room. He still had that mean look in his eye. He was remembering the toothbrush. 'What's going on now?' he asked in a black voice.

'Nothing,' I said. 'I was just thanking Mum for making me these nice underpants.' I pulled on the fairy pants and quickly covered them up with my jeans. At least no one else would know I had them on. That was one thing to be thankful for.

The underpants felt strange. They made me tingle all over. And my head felt light. There was something not quite right about those underpants – and I am not talking about the fairies.

3

I had breakfast and went out to the front gate. Pete was waiting for me. He is my best mate; we always walk to school together. 'Have you got your running shoes?' he asked.

'Oh no,' I groaned. 'I forgot. It's the cross country race today.' I went back and got my running shoes. I came back out walking very slowly. I was thinking about the race. I would have to go to the changing rooms and get changed in front of Scrag Murphy and all the other boys. They would all laugh their heads off when they saw my fairy underpants.

We walked through the park on the way to school. There was a big lake in the middle. 'Let's chuck some stones,' said Pete. 'See who can throw the furthest.' I didn't even answer. I was feeling weak in the stomach. 'What's the matter with you?' he asked. 'You look like death warmed up.'

I looked around. There was no one else in the park. 'Look at this,' I said. I undid my fly and showed Pete the underpants. His eyes bugged out like organ stops; then he started to laugh. He fell over on the grass and laughed his silly head off. Tears rolled down his cheeks. He really thought it was funny. Some friend.

After a while Pete stopped laughing. 'You poor thing,' he said. 'What are you going to do? Scrag Murphy and the others will never let you forget it.'

We started throwing stones into the lake. I didn't try very hard. My heart wasn't in it. 'Hey,' said Pete. 'That was a good shot. It went right over to the other side.' He was right. The stone had reached the other side of the lake. No one had ever done that before; it was too far.

I picked up another stone. This time I threw as hard as I could. The stone went right over the lake and disappeared over some trees. 'Wow,' yelled Pete. 'That's the best shot I've ever seen. No one can throw that far.' He looked at me in a funny way.

7

My skin was all tingling. 'I feel strong,' I said. 'I feel as if I can do anything.' I went over to a park bench. It was a large concrete one. I lifted it up with one hand. I held it high over my head. I couldn't believe it.

Pete just stood there with his mouth hanging open. He couldn't believe it either. I felt great. I jumped for joy. I sailed high into the air. I went up three metres. 'What a jump,' yelled Pete.

My skin was still tingling. Especially under the under-pants. 'It's the underpants,' I said. 'The underpants are giving me strength.' I grinned. 'They are not underpants. They are *wunderpants*.'

'Super Jocks,' said Pete. We both started cackling like a couple of hens. We laughed until our sides ached.

4

I told Pete not to tell anyone about the wunderpants. We decided to keep it a secret. Nothing much happened until the cross country race that afternoon. All the boys went to the changing room to put on their running gear. Scrag Murphy was there. I tried to get into my shorts without him seeing my wunderpants, but it was no good. He noticed them as soon as I dropped my jeans.

'Ah ha,' he shouted. 'Look at baby britches. Look at his fairy pants.' Everyone looked. They all started to laugh. How embarrassing. They were all looking at the fairies on my wunderpants.

Scrag Murphy was a big, fat bloke. He was really tough. He came over and pulled the elastic on my wunderpants. Then he let it go. 'Ouch,' I said. 'Cut that out. That hurts.'

'What's the matter, little Diddums?' he said. 'Can't

you take it?' He shoved me roughly against the wall. I wasn't going to let him get away with that, so I pushed him back – just a little push. He went flying across the room and crashed into the wall on the other side. I just didn't know my own strength. That little push had sent him all that way. It was the wunderpants.

Scrag Murphy looked at me with shock and surprise that soon turned to a look of hate. But he didn't say anything. No one said anything. They were all thinking I was going to get my block knocked off next time I saw Scrag Murphy.

About forty kids were running in the race. We had to run through the countryside, following markers that had been put out by the teachers. It was a hot day, so I decided to wear a pair of shorts but no top.

As soon as the starting gun went I was off like a flash. I had kept my wunderpants on and they were working really well. I went straight out to the front. I had never run so fast before. As I ran along the road I passed a man on a bike. He tried to keep up with me, but he couldn't. Then I passed a car. This was really something. This was great.

I looked behind. None of the others were in sight – I was miles ahead. The trail turned off the road and into the bush. I was running along a narrow track in the forest. After a while I came to a small creek. I was hot so I decided to have a dip. After all, the others were a long way behind; I had plenty of time. I took off my shorts and running shoes, but I left the wunderpants on. I wasn't going to part with them.

I dived into the cold water. It was refreshing. I lay on my back looking at the sky. Life was good. These wunderpants were terrific. I would never be scared of Scrag Murphy while I had them on.

Then something started to happen – something terrible. The wunderpants started to get tight. They hurt. They were shrinking. They were shrinking smaller and smaller. The pain was awful. I had to get them off. I struggled and wriggled; they were so tight they cut into my skin. In the end I got them off, and only just in time. They shrank so small that they would only just fit over my thumb. I had a narrow escape. I could have been killed by the shrinking wunderpants.

Just then I heard voices coming. It was the others in the race. I was trapped – I couldn't get out to put on my shorts. There were girls in the race. I had to stay in the middle of the creek in the nude.

5

It took quite a while for all the others to run by. They were all spread out along the track. Every time I went to get out of the pool, someone else would come. After a while Pete stopped at the pool. 'What are you doing?' he said. 'Even super jocks won't help you win from this far back.'

'Keep going,' I said. 'I'll tell you about it later.' I didn't want to tell him that I was in the nude. Some girls were with him.

Pete and the girls took off along the track. A bit later the last runner arrived. It was Scrag Murphy. He couldn't run fast – he was carrying too much weight. 'Well, look at this,' he said. 'It's little Fairy Pants. And what's this we have here?' He picked up my shorts and running shoes from the bank of the creek. Then he ran off with them.

'Come back,' I screamed. 'Bring those back here.' He didn't take any notice. He just laughed and kept running.

I didn't know what to do. I didn't have a stitch of clothing. I didn't even have any shoes. I was starting to feel cold; the water was freezing. I was covered in goose pimples and my teeth were chattering. In the end I had to get out. I would have frozen to death if I stayed in the water any longer.

I went and sat on a rock in the sun and tried to think of a way to get home without being seen. It was all right in the bush. I could always hide behind a tree if someone came. But once I reached the road I would be in trouble; I couldn't just walk along the road in the nude.

Then I had an idea. I looked at the tiny underpants. I couldn't put them on, but they still might work. I put them over my thumb and jumped. It was no good. It was just an ordinary small jump. I picked up a stone and threw it. It only went a short way, not much of a throw at all. The pants were too small, and I was my weak old self again.

I lay down on the rock in the sun. Ants started to crawl over me. Then the sun went behind a cloud. I started to get cold, but I couldn't walk home – not in the raw. I felt miserable. I looked around for something to wear, but there was nothing. Just trees, bushes and grass.

I knew I would have to wait until dark. The others would all have gone home by now. Pete would think I had gone home, and my parents would think I was at his place. No one was going to come and help me.

I started to think about Scrag Murphy. He was going to pay for this. I would get him back somehow.

11

Time went slowly, but at last it started to grow dark. I made my way back along the track. I was in bare feet and I kept standing on stones. Branches reached out and scratched me in all sorts of painful places. Then I started to think about snakes. What if I stood on one?

There were all sorts of noises in the dark. The moon had gone in, and it was hard to see where I was going. I have to admit it: I was scared. Scared stiff. To cheer myself up I started to think about what I was going to do to Scrag Murphy. Boy, was he going to get it.

At last I came to the road. I was glad to be out of the bush. My feet were cut and bleeding and I hobbled along. Every time a car went by I had to dive into the bushes. I couldn't let myself get caught in the headlights of the cars.

I wondered what I was going to do when I reached the town. There might be people around. I broke off a branch from a bush and held it in front of my 'you know what'. It was prickly, but it was better than nothing.

By the time I reached the town it was late. There was no one around. But I had to be careful – someone might come out of a house at any minute. I ran from tree to tree and wall to wall, hiding in the shadows as I went. Lucky for me the moon was in and it was very dark.

Then I saw something that gave me an idea – a phone box. I opened the door and stepped inside. A dim light shone on my naked body. I hoped that no one was looking. I had no money, but Pete had told me that if you yell into the ear-piece they can hear you on the other end. It was worth a try. I dialled our home number. Dad anwered. 'Yes,' he said.

'I'm in the nude,' I shouted. 'I've lost my clothes. Help. Help.'

'Hello, hello. Who's there?' said Dad.

I shouted at the top of my voice, but Dad just kept saying 'Hello'. He sounded cross. Then I heard him say to Mum, 'It's probably that boy up to his tricks again.' He hung up the phone.

I decided to make a run for it. It was the only way. I dropped my bush and started running. I went for my life. I reached our street without meeting a soul. I thought I was safe, but I was wrong. I crashed right into someone and sent them flying. It was old Mrs Jeeves from across the road.

'Sorry,' I said. 'Gee, I'm sorry.' I helped her stand up. She was a bit short sighted and it was dark. She hadn't noticed that I didn't have any clothes on. Then the moon came out – the blazing moon. I tried to cover my nakedness with my hands, but it was no good.

'Disgusting,' she screeched. 'Disgusting. I'll tell your father about this.'

I ran home as fast as I could. I went in the back door and jumped into bed. I tried to pretend that I was asleep. Downstairs I could hear Mrs Jeeves yelling at Dad; then the front door closed. I heard his footsteps coming up the stairs.

6

Well, I really copped it. I was in big trouble. Dad went on and on. 'What are you thinking of, lad? Running around in the nude. Losing all your clothes. What will the neighbours think?' He went on like that for about a week. I couldn't tell him the truth – he wouldn't believe it. No one would. The only ones who knew the whole story were Pete and I.

Dad grounded me for a month. I wasn't allowed out of

13

the house except to go to school. No pictures, no swimming, nothing. And no pocket money either.

It was a bad month. Very bad indeed. At school Scrag Murphy gave me a hard time. He called me 'Fairy Pants'. Every one thought it was a great joke, and there was nothing I could do about it. He was just too big for me, and his mates were all tough guys.

'This is serious,' said Pete. 'We have to put Scrag Murphy back in his box. They are starting to call me 'Friend Of Fairy Pants' now. We have to get even.'

We thought and thought but we couldn't come up with anything. Then I remembered the mouse race in Smith's barn. 'We will win the mouse race,' I shouted. 'It's in a month's time. We can use the next month to train my mouse.'

'That's it,' said Pete. 'The prize is fifty dollars. Scrag Murphy thinks he is going to win. It will really get up his nose if we take off the prize.'

I went and fetched Swift Sam. 'He's small,' I said. 'But he's fast. I bet he can beat Murphy's mouse. It's called Mugger.'

We started to train Swift Sam. Every day after school we took him around a track in the back yard. We tied a piece of cheese on the end of a bit of string. Swift Sam chased after it as fast as he could. After six laps we gave him the piece of cheese to eat. At the start he could do six laps in ten minutes. By the end of the month he was down to three minutes.

'Scrag Murphy, look out,' said Pete with a grin. 'We are really going to beat the pants off you this time.'

The day of the big race came at last. There were about one hundred kids in Smith's barn. No adults knew about it – they would probably have stopped it if they knew. It cost fifty cents to get in. That's where the prize money came from. A kid called Tiger Gleeson took up the money and gave out the prize at the end. He was the organiser of the whole thing.

Scrag Murphy was there, of course. 'It's in the bag,' he swaggered. 'Mugger can't lose. I've fed him on a special diet. He is the fittest mouse in the county. He will eat Swift Sam, just you wait and see.'

I didn't say anything. But I was very keen to see his mouse, Mugger. Scrag Murphy had it in a box. No one had seen it yet.

'Right,' said Tiger. 'Get out your mice.' I put Swift Sam down on the track. He looked very small. He started sniffing around. I hoped he would run as fast with the other mice there – he hadn't had any match practice before. Then the others put their mice on the track. Everyone except Scrag Murphy. He still had Mugger in the box.

Scrag Murphy put his hand in the box and took out Mugger. He was the biggest mouse I had ever seen. He was at least ten times as big as Swift Sam. 'Hey,' said Pete. 'That's not a mouse. That's a rat. You can't race a rat. It's not fair.'

'It's not a rat,' said Scrag Murphy in a threatening voice. 'It's just a big mouse. I've been feeding it up'. I looked at it again. It was a rat all right. It was starting to attack the mice.

'We will take a vote,' said Tiger. 'All those that

think it is a rat, put your hands up.' He counted all the hands.

'Fifty,' he said. 'Now all those who say that Mugger is a mouse put your hands up.' He counted again.

'Fifty two. Mugger is a mouse.'

Scrag Murphy and his gang started to cheer. He had brought all his mates with him. It was a put-up job.

'Right,' said Tiger Gleeson. 'Get ready to race.'

8

There were about ten mice in the race – or I should say nine mice and one rat. Two rats if you counted Scrag Murphy. All the owners took out their string and cheese. 'Go,' shouted Tiger Gleeson.

Mugger jumped straight on to a little mouse next to him and bit it on the neck. The poor thing fell over and lay still. 'Boo,' yelled some of the crowd.

Swift Sam ran to the front straight away. He was going really well. Then Mugger started to catch up. It was neck and neck for five laps. First Mugger would get in front, then Swift Sam. Everyone in the barn went crazy. They were yelling their heads off.

By the sixth lap Mugger started to fall behind. All the other mice were not in the race. They had been lapped twice by Mugger and Swift Sam. But Mugger couldn't keep up with Swift Sam; he was about a tail behind. Suddenly something terrible happened. Mugger jumped onto Swift Sam's tail and grabbed it in his teeth. The crowd started to boo. Even Scrag Murphy's mates were booing.

But Swift Sam kept going. He didn't stop for a second. He just pulled that great rat along after him. It rolled over and over behind the little mouse. Mugger held on for grim death, but he couldn't stop Swift Sam. 'What a mouse,' screamed the crowd as Swift Sam crossed the finish line still towing Mugger behind him.

Scrag Murphy stormed off out of the barn. He didn't even take Mugger with him. Tiger handed me the fifty dollars. Then he held up Swift Sam. 'Swift Sam is the winner,' he said. 'The only mouse in the world with its own little pair of fairy underpants.'

LICKED

1

Tomorrow when Dad calms down I'll own up. Tell him the truth. He might laugh. He might cry. He might strangle me. But I have to put him out of his misery.

I like my dad. He takes me fishing. He gives me arm wrestles in front of the fire on cold nights. He plays Scrabble instead of watching the news. He tries practical jokes on me. And he keeps his promises. Always.

But he has two faults. Bad faults. One is to do with flies. He can't stand them. If there's a fly in the room he has to kill it. He won't use fly spray because of the ozone layer so he chases them with a fly swat. He races around the house swiping and swatting like a mad thing. He won't stop until the fly is flat. Squashed. Squished – sometimes still squirming on the end of the fly swat.

He's a dead-eye shot. He hardly ever misses. When his old fly swat was almost worn out I bought him a nice new yellow one for his birthday. It wasn't yellow for long. It soon had bits of fly smeared all over it.

It's funny the different colours that squashed flies have

inside them. Mostly it is black or brown. But often there are streaks of runny red stuff and sometimes bits of blue. The wings flash like diamonds if you hold them up to the light. But mostly the wings fall off unless they are stuck to the swat with a bit of squashed innards.

2

Chasing flies is Dad's first fault. His second one is table manners. He is mad about manners.

And it is always my manners that are the matter.

'Andrew,' he says. 'Don't put your elbows on the table.'

'Don't talk with your mouth full.'

'Don't lick your fingers.'

'Don't dunk your biscuit in the coffee.'

This is the way he goes on every meal time. He has a thing about flies and a thing about manners.

Anyway, to get back to the story. One day Dad is peeling the potatoes for tea. I am looking for my fifty cents that rolled under the table about a week ago. Mum is cutting up the cabbage and talking to Dad. They do not know that I am there. It is a very important meal because Dad's boss, Mr Spinks, is coming for tea. Dad never stops going on about my manners when someone comes for tea.

'You should stop picking on Andrew at tea time,' says Mum.

'I don't,' says Dad.

'Yes you do,' says Mum. 'It's always "don't do this, don't do that." You'll give the boy a complex.'

I have never heard of a complex before but I guess that it is something awful like pimples.

20

'Tonight,' says Mum. 'I want you to go for the whole meal without telling Andrew off once.'

'Easy,' says Dad.

'Try hard,' says Mum, 'Promise me that you won't get cross with him.'

Dad looks at her for a long time. 'Okay,' he says. 'It's a deal. I won't say one thing about his manners. But you're not allowed to either. What's good for me is good for you.'

'Shake,' says Mum. They shake hands and laugh.

I find the fifty cents and sneak out. I take a walk down the street to spend it before tea. Dad has promised not to tell me off at tea time. I think about how I can make him crack. It should be easy. I will slurp my soup. He hates that. He will tell me off. He might even yell. I just know that he can't go for the whole meal without going crook. 'This is going to be fun,' I say to myself.

3

That night Mum sets the table with the new tablecloth. And the best knives and forks. And the plates that I am not allowed to touch. She puts out serviettes in little rings. All of this means that it is an important meal. We don't usually use serviettes.

Mr Spinks comes in his best suit. He wears gold glasses and he frowns a lot. I can tell that he doesn't like children. You can always tell when adults don't like kids. They smile at you with their lips but not with their eyes.

Anyway, we sit down to tea. I put my secret weapon on the floor under the table. I'm sure that I can make Dad

21

crack without using it. But it is there if all else fails.

The first course is soup and bread rolls. I make loud slurping noises with the soup. No one says anything about it. I make the slurping noises longer and louder. They go on and on and on. It sounds like someone has pulled the plug out of the bath. Dad clears his throat but doesn't say anything.

I try something different. I dip my bread in the soup and make it soggy. Then I hold it high above my head and drop it down into my mouth. I catch it with a loud slopping noise. I try again with an even bigger bit. This time I miss my mouth and the bit of soupy bread hits me in the eye.

Nothing is said. Dad looks at me. Mum looks at me. Mr Spinks tries not to look at me. They are talking about how Dad might get a promotion at work. They are pretending that I am not revolting.

The next course is chicken. Dad will crack over the chicken. He'll say something. He hates me picking up the bones.

The chicken is served. 'I've got the chicken's bottom,' I say in a loud voice.

Dad glares at me but he doesn't answer. I pick up the chicken and start stuffing it into my mouth with my fingers. I grab a roast potato and break it in half. I dip my fingers into the margarine and put some on the potato. It runs all over the place.

I have never seen anyone look as mad as the way Dad looks at me. He glares. He stares. He clears his throat. But still he doesn't crack. What a man. Nothing can make him break his promise.

I snap a chicken bone in half and suck out the middle.

It is hollow and I can see right through it. I suck and slurp and swallow. Dad is going red in the face. Little veins are standing out on his nose. But still he does not crack.

The last course is baked apple and custard. I will get him with that. Mr Spinks has stopped talking about Dad's promotion. He is discussing something about discipline. About setting limits. About insisting on standards. Something like that. I put the hollow bone into the custard and use it like a straw. I suck the custard up the hollow chicken bone.

Dad clears his throat. He is very red in the face. 'Andrew,' he says.

He is going to crack. I have won.

'Yes,' I say through a mouth full of custard.

'Nothing,' he mumbles.

Dad is terrific. He is under enormous pressure but still he keeps his cool. There is only one thing left to do. I take out my secret weapon.

4

I place the yellow fly swat on the table next to my knife.

Everyone looks at it lying there on the white tablecloth. They stare and stare and stare. But nothing is said.

I pick up the fly swat and start to lick it. I lick it like an ice cream. A bit of chewy, brown goo comes off on my tongue. I swallow it quickly. Then I crunch a bit of crispy, black stuff.

Mr Spinks rushes out to the kitchen. I can hear him being sick in the kitchen sink.

Dad stands up. It is too much for him. He cracks. 'Aaaaaagh,' he screams. He charges at me with hands held out like claws.

I run for it. I run down to my room and lock the door. Dad yells and shouts. He kicks and screams. But I lie low.

Tomorrow, when he calms down, I'll own up. I'll tell him how I went down the street and bought a new fly swat for fifty cents. I'll tell him about the currants and little bits of licorice that I smeared on the fly swat.

I mean, I wouldn't really eat dead flies. Not unless it was for something important anyway.

RINGING WET

1

The man next door buried his wife in the backyard.

That's what I reckon, anyway. Dad says I have a vivid imagination. And my rotten, horrible, worst-ever big brother says I am nuts.

But I am not nuts. No way. See, it starts like this. I am reading a book where five kids go on a holiday. They discover smugglers in some underground caves but the adults won't believe them. Everyone thinks they are crazy. But in the end they catch the smugglers and become heroes. All the parents and police have to say sorry.

Since I read that book I have been on the lookout. To be honest there are not many smugglers around our way. I have looked and looked. There are not even any underground tunnels.

But there is Mr Grunge next door. He moved in two months ago. He acts in a very suspicious way. Consider these facts:

1. Mr Grunge has a crabby face.
2. He never comes out in the daytime.
3. He shouts at his wife in a loud, horrible voice.
4. His wife does all of the shopping and washing-up and cooking.
5. Mr Grunge just sits there all day watching TV.
6. Two days ago Mrs Grunge disappears.
   Yes, DISAPPEARS.
7. The night that his wife disappears Mr Grunge digs in the backyard.
   Yes, DIGS IN THE GARDEN *AT NIGHT*.

I know all this because I have been spying on them through a chink in their curtains.

Yes, it all fits in. They have an argument. He hits her with the frying-pan or something. Then he drags her out into the backyard. He takes off her diamond bracelet and buries her. I do not actually see this happen. But I put two and two together. It is the only explanation.

'Don't be crazy, Misty,' says Dad. 'She's probably gone on a holiday.'

'In the middle of winter?' I say.

'She could have gone to Queensland to get a bit of sun,' says Dad.

'Without her best diamond bracelet?' I say.

Dad looks at me through narrow eyes. 'How do you know she hasn't taken her bracelet?' he says.

'She's been peeping through the window,' says Simon, my rotten worst-ever brother.

Dad bangs down his paper on the table. He is as mad as a hatter. 'Misty,' he yells. 'That is a terrible thing to do. Spying and going into someone else's garden.'

Simon is such a dobber. He always spoils things. He is a real wet blanket. I decide to pay him back. 'Well, *he* got a detention at school yesterday,' I yell. 'For not doing his homework.'

Dad is really mad now. He rolls his eyes. 'What a way to start the school holidays,' he roars. 'Go to your rooms at once. Both of you.'

I stomp off to my bedroom and almost slam the door. There is an exact amount of noise you can make when you are almost slamming the door. If you do it too loud your parents will stop your pocket money for a month. If you get it right they cannot be quite sure that you actually slammed the door and they won't do anything. But it still annoys them.

My Dad is so stubborn. So is Simon. They won't believe that Mr Grunge has buried his wife in the garden. There is only one thing for me to do. One night, when there is no moon. When it is very dark. I will go and dig her up. Yes, DIG HER UP.

2

I am lying there in bed thinking about how I will dig up the body when Simon bursts into the room. He has his fingers held out like claws. 'Ticky, ticky, ticky,' he says with a nasty look on his face.

'No, Simon. No, no, no,' I scream. 'Not that. Don't. Please, please. I'm sorry I dobbed.'

'Ticky, ticky, ticky,' says Simon. Oh, he is so awful. He is bigger than me. Almost as big as Dad. I just can't stand up to him. I curl up in a ball on the bed. It is my only defence.

Simon gets his horrible fingers in under my armpits and starts to tickle. I hate it. I just hate it. I start to scream and kick and yell. 'Don't,' I yell. 'You pain. Dad, Dad, Dad.' I stop yelling. I am laughing. I don't want to laugh. I want to scream. But his fingers are digging in and I just can't help it.

I squirm and kick. And then I do it. I knew I would do it. And so did Simon. It is why he is tickling me. I always do it when someone tickles me.

I wet my pants. Yes, WET MY PANTS. Warm wet wee runs down my legs and onto the bed. Oh, it is terrible.

Simon sees. 'What's that?' he mocks. 'Where did that come from?' He laughs wickedly and then runs out the door.

I throw a pillow after him. 'You wait,' I say. 'You just wait.'

I hang my head in my hands. I am so ashamed. I always wet myself when someone tickles me. Even if I just get excited I do it. The doctor says I will grow out of it. Probably I will. By the time I am fifty.

There is something else, too. Even worse. Every night I wet the bed. It is awful. Just awful. In the mornings I wake up and everything is wet. I hate it.

I hate it. I hate it. I hate it.

Last year I couldn't go on the school camp. I was just too embarrassed.

I have a shower and change my clothes. Then I go into the lounge to see Dad. 'Something has to be done,' I say. 'Can't you do something to stop this bed-wetting? It is ruining my life.'

Dad nods his head. 'There is one more thing to try,' he says. 'I have been hoping we wouldn't need it. But I guess we have to give it a go.'

'Anything,' I say. 'I will try anything.'

3

That night Dad comes home with a rubber blanket. 'We put this under your sheet,' says Dad. 'When you wee it makes the blanket wet and it will ring a bell. You wake up and we change the sheets. After a couple of weeks your brain knows what is going to happen and it stops you wetting. Bingo – you are cured.'

I don't like the sound of it. Not one bit. But I am desperate. I will try anything. I snuggle down under the covers. Outside the moon is shining bright. It is not dark enough to go and dig in the neighbour's garden. So I close my eyes and drop off to sleep.

'Ding, ding, ding, ding.' Good grief. What is it? That terrible noise. I sit bolt upright in bed. It is like sirens from the police, the ambulance and the fire brigade all put together. My head is spinning. Is the house on fire or what?

I know. I know. I bet the police have come to arrest Mr Grunge. They will charge him with murder.

Dad bursts into the room with a smile. 'It works,' he says. 'Out you hop, sweetheart. You go and change your pyjamas and I'll put on fresh sheets.'

My heart sinks. It is not the police. I have wet the bed. The terrible noise comes from the bell attached to the rubber blanket. It works all right. It is the worst noise in the world.

Dad makes the bed while I put on dry pyjamas. 'See, that wasn't so bad,' says Dad as he walks out. He is quite chirpy really.

I snuggle down under the clean, crisp sheets. I am so tired. This getting up in the middle of the night takes it out of you. I have no sooner closed my eyes than 'ding, ding, ding, ding'. Oh no. I've wet the bed again. I look at the clock. Two hours. Have two hours really passed already?

Dad staggers into the room. This time he is not so chirpy. 'Geeze,' he says. 'I'd just dropped off to sleep. Okay, up you get. I'll get some dry sheets.' Dad is not exactly cross. Well, he is trying not to be cross. But I can tell that he does not like getting up in the middle of the night. And he is not the only one – that's for sure.

The next day is Saturday. It is Mum's weekend. Mum and Dad split up a couple of years ago and we live with Dad. Every second Saturday we go off with Mum. It is grouse because she takes us to lots of good places. To be honest, though, I wish she still lived at home.

Dad looks out of the window. 'Here's your mother,' he says. He never calls her Mum any more. He always calls her *your mother*. Funny that. Anyway, Simon and I race out and hop into Mum's car.

'Where are we going?' says Simon.

'Luna Park,' says Mum.

'Unreal,' we both yell.

We wander through the great big mouth that is the entrance to Luna Park and look around. We have a ride on the Big Dipper, the Water Caves and go into the Giggle Palace. They are all great.

'Let's go on the Rotor,' says Simon.

'What's that?' says Mum.

'It's this round room,' I say. 'You stick to the wall. I am not going on it. No way.'

'Neither am I,' says Mum.

'Wimps,' says Simon. 'I'm going on it. You can watch if you like. You can go upstairs and look down on the brave ones.' He bends one arm and bulges out his muscle. He thinks he is so tough.

4

We all get in the line, pay our money and file inside. The line splits into two. One line is for the people who are going to stick to the wall. The other is for those who want to watch. There is a lot of pushing and shoving and Mum is not sure where we are. 'You go in there,' says Simon.

Mum and I file through a door while Simon heads up some stairs. The door slams behind us. We look around. We are in a big, round room with about ten others. There are a whole lot of people up above looking down on us. It is sort of like a round squash court with spectators sitting around upstairs.

What is going on here? What has happened?

Simon has tricked us. That's what. I see his grinning face peering down from the spectators' seats. He thinks he is so smart. He has sent us into the wrong place. We are inside the Rotor. Yes, INSIDE.

I start to panic. I have to get out of here. I just have to. But where is the door? I can't even see it. There is no handle. And the walls are covered in rubber.

A loud voice comes over the microphone. 'All riders stand against the wall, please,' it says. Riders? I am not meant to be a rider. I am meant to be a watcher. 'Let me out,' I yell.

But it is too late. Mum drags me back to the wall and the room starts to spin. Faster and faster. The faces up above are just a blur. We are whirling around like a crazy spinning top. Suddenly the floor drops away. And we are stuck to the wall. Right up in the air.

This is terrible. Horrible. I am scared. I'm embarrassed. Everyone is looking at us. We are like flies on the wall.

Mum starts to squirm. She has turned sideways. If she is not careful she will soon be upside down. Some of the people on the wall are groaning. Others are screaming. Some are laughing and having fun.

But I am not having fun. I am excited. When I am excited something terrible always happens.

And it does happen. Oh, horror of horrors. It happens. I wet my pants.

There on the wall with everyone looking – I wet my pants.

A river of warm wet wee runs along the wall. It snakes its way towards Mum. My shame scribbles its hateful way across the round, spinning room.

I close my eyes and try to pretend that this is not happening. But it is.

After ages and ages the walls start to slow. Gradually the floor comes up to meet us. Finally the Rotor stops and I am standing on the floor in front of a wet, smeared wall. My legs and dress are all wet. Mum and I stagger outside and blink in the sunlight.

Simon is going to die. Simon is history. I will get him for this.

Before I can reach Simon to strangle him, Mum grabs him by the shoulders and shakes him until his head just about drops off. 'You have ruined the day,' she yells. 'Now I will have to take you back to your father's so that Misty can change.'

We all drive home without talking. I am so angry. 'I will get you for this, Simon,' I think to myself. 'I will get you for this. If it is the last thing I do, I will pay you back.'

5

Mum drops us at the gate and drives off. As we walk up the drive I see Dad's startled face staring out of the window. I also see Mr Grunge in his backyard. He has a shovel in his hand. He stares at me as I go by. It is almost like he can read my mind. I shiver and hurry indoors.

Dad is surprised to see us. 'What are you doing back so soon?' he says. He is annoyed. And I know why. In the lounge-room is his girlfriend, Brook. She only ever comes over when we are out. Her hair is all ruffled and she looks embarrassed. Dad's shirt is hanging out. They have been cuddling. Yes, CUDDLING. And we have broken it up.

I am annoyed too. He should be pleased to see us back. Not annoyed.

'Simon made me wet my pants,' I yell.

'I did not,' he says.

'Liar, liar, liar,' I shout.

Dad rolls his eyeballs at Brook. Then he does something strange. He takes out his wallet. He bangs a fifty-dollar note down on the table. 'See this?' he says. 'This is for the person who keeps quiet the longest.'

Simon and I stop yelling. We are both very interested.

'The first one to speak,' says Dad, 'does not get the fifty-dollar note. As soon as one of you speaks, the other one gets this. Do you understand?'

I open my mouth to say 'yes'. But I don't. No way. I just nod my head in silence. So does Simon.

'Not one word,' says Dad. 'Not a shout, not a scream, not a giggle. Total silence. That is the deal. Get it?'

We both nod our heads again.

Dad looks smug. 'Now maybe we will get some peace at last,' he says.

I grin an evil grin. Now I will get Simon back. I will win the fifty dollars and he will be really cut. It is perfect. He might be bigger than me. He might be stronger. He might even be smarter. But I am stubborn. I will not say a word to anyone. Even if it takes ten years.

That night I get into bed and wriggle down under the blankets. I turn off the lights and my mind starts to wander. Mr Grunge was giving me a funny look this afternoon. What was he thinking about? Suddenly I feel cold all over.

He knows.

He knows that I know that he has buried his wife in the backyard.

What if I am next?

I can't sleep. I toss and turn. Finally I drift off when . . . 'crash'. My bedroom door flies open. Someone bursts into the room. My brain freezes with fear. It is a person wearing a devil's mask. A horrible, horrible mask. The figure dances around at the end of my bed.

Suddenly I am not scared any more. I have seen that mask before. Simon bought it at the Show. He is trying to make me scream. He wants me to yell out. So that he can get the money. But it won't work. I turn on the light and take out a pencil and paper. 'Buzz off, Simon,' I write in large letters.

Simon pulls off the mask and pulls a face at me. Then he leaves.

6

It takes me ages and ages but finally I fall off to sleep.

'Ding, ding, ding, ding.' What, what, what? Rats. It is the bed-wetting alarm again. Already. What a racket. It's enough to wake the dead.

Dad comes in and turns on the light. He holds a finger up to his lips. 'Don't say a word,' he says. 'Remember the fifty dollars.' He sure is taking this seriously.

I put on a clean pair of pyjamas and Dad changes the sheets. Then he goes off to bed. Brook must have gone home.

An hour ticks by. And then another. I just can't get off to sleep. Too much has happened. I have wet my pants on the Rotor. Dad was cross because we came home early.

Simon is a horrible worst-ever brother. Mr Grunge knows that I am on to him. My life is a total mess.

If only I was rich or beautiful or famous.

Outside it is dark. There is no moon.

Famous.

That's it. Tonight is the night. I will sneak out into Mr Grunge's garden. I will dig up his wife before he can come and get me. I will be famous. I bet there will be a reward. And it will be worth at least fifty dollars. Maybe more.

I get dressed, push up the window and sneak out into the night. Down to the shed for a shovel. Up over the fence. This is easy. It is dark. Very dark.

The garden is as silent as a graveyard. A little shiver runs up my spine. This is not easy. This is scary. Where is the grave? Where is the spot where Mr Grunge has buried Mrs Grunge? Where is Mr Grunge?

I feel my way around. Gradually my eyes grow used to the dark. There it is. Over there. Crafty. What a crafty devil. He has planted tomato plants on top of the grave. And tied them up to stakes. He is trying to make everyone think it is just a vegetable garden. But he can't fool me. I know it is a grave.

Graves are spooky things. Maybe this is not such a good idea. What if Mr Grunge is nearby? Watching. Waiting. I peep over my shoulder. What was that? Nothing. Terrible thoughts enter my mind. If Mr Grunge catches me I will be history. What will he plant on *my* grave?

Run, run, run for it. No, stay. You will never sleep at night until this mystery is solved. I lean over the vegetable garden. I take a deep breath and rip out the little seedlings and the stakes. Then I start to dig.

36

It is slow, hard work. As I dig I start to think. What will I find? What if I suddenly uncover a horrible white hand? What if I hit a nose? What if there are staring, dead eyes down there? With dirt in them.

I dig more and more slowly. I don't want to find Mrs Grunge. But I do, too. I am so scared. There is a rustle in the bushes. What was that?

'Aargh,' I scream. Eyes. Someone's eyes. Staring at me from the bushes.

I drop my shovel and run. I scream and scream and scream. I am up and over that fence before you can blink. I am through that window and back into bed before you can snap your fingers.

I have my eyes closed. I want to fall asleep. And quickly. There is going to be big trouble. I can feel it in my bones.

7

There is a knock on the front door. I hear footsteps. I hear the front door open. I hear voices. Oh no. This is terrible. I have had it.

Footsteps approach my bedroom. Someone comes into the room and turns on the light. I pretend to be asleep but through my closed eyelashes I see Dad. He is carrying a shovel. He is looking at the open window. 'I know you're awake, Misty,' he says. 'Come with me.'

Dad pulls me out of bed towards the lounge-room. 'Mr Grunge is here,' he says. 'Someone has gone and ruined his tomato patch. A vandal has dug it up.'

I pull my hand away from Dad and tear back to the

bedroom. I grab a bit of paper and a pencil. 'He murdered his wife,' I write. 'I was digging her up.'

Dad reads the note and throws it onto the floor. Then he drags me into the lounge. 'This is Mr Grunge,' says Dad. Mr Grunge is sitting there on the sofa. He is not saying anything. He is staring at me with evil eyes. Why can't Dad see it? Anyone would know that Mr Grunge was a murderer just by looking at him.

I open my mouth to speak. I open my mouth to tell Dad to call the police. That will prove it once and for all. They can dig up the vegetable patch.

But I do not get a chance to say anything. Dad goes on and on and on. Talk about trouble. Boy, do I cop it. I am a vandal. I am hopeless. I am mean. I am ungrateful. I will have to plant out a new garden. Just when Dad is starting to get some happiness in his life, I ruin everything. It seems like the lecture will never end. I start to cry. Silent tears run down my cheeks. In the end Dad feels sorry for me and sends me off to bed.

I hear Dad and Mr Grunge talking in the lounge. The front door slams. I look out of the window and see Mr Grunge walking down the front path. 'Murderer,' I think to myself. I just know that Mrs Grunge is dead and buried in the vegetable patch.

But no one will believe me.

Why doesn't anything nice ever happen to me? Why does everything have to go wrong?

There is only one good thing about the whole episode.

I didn't say a word. I didn't even cry out loud. I am still in the running for the fifty dollars. I will get that fifty dollars and pay Simon back if it kills me.

Once again I try to fall off to sleep. More hours tick by but sleep won't come. My mind is too full of misery.

Suddenly I hear something. A rustle outside. There is someone in the garden.

And my window is still open. Yes, MY WINDOW IS STILL OPEN.

The skin seems to crawl over my bones. I am shivering with fear. What is outside? Who is outside?

It is him. I just know it is him. It is Mr Grunge. My throat is dry. I am petrified with fear. He is coming. He is coming. He is coming.

A dark figure appears at the window. A figure wearing a balaclava. The intruder puts a leg through the window. I open my mouth to scream out, 'Dad, Dad, Dad.'

But I don't call out. I don't say a word.

My heart is beating like a million hammers. I am so scared. But I am not stupid. My mind is working over-time. Because of the balaclava I don't really know who it is. This could be Simon again. It could be him trying to make me call out for Dad. So that he can get the fifty dollars.

Oh, what will I do? If it is Mr Grunge I will end up in the vegetable patch. But if it is Simon I will lose the bet when I call out. And he will get the money.

What will I do? What, what what?

I know. Suddenly it comes to me. I know what to do.

And I do it. Yes, I do it.

ON PURPOSE.

I wet my pants. Wonderful warm wee runs down between my legs.

'Ding, ding, ding, ding.' What a racket. It is like sirens

from the police, the ambulance and the fire brigade all put together.

The intruder straightens up with a jerk, bangs into the window and slumps to the ground – out like a light.

Dad bursts into the room. 'What in the . . . ?' he says. Then he sees the figure on the floor. We stare down. Who is under that balaclava? Is it Simon? Or is it Mr Grunge? Is it a man or is it a boy?

Dad bends down and pulls up the balaclava. We both stare with wide open eyes. It is not a man. And it is not a boy.

Just then Simon bursts into the room and looks at the burglar.

'Mrs Grunge,' he yells.

Yes, *MRS* GRUNGE. She is not dead. She is not buried. She is out like a light on the floor. Her diamond bracelet glints in the moonlight.

I am still sitting up in my wet bed. Okay, I was wrong. Mrs Grunge is not buried in the garden. She is not dead. I made a mistake. But I grin. Something good has happened.

'You spoke first,' I say to my rotten worst-ever, wet-blanket brother.

Simon looks as if his face is going to fall off. He is so cut.

Well, after that everything is fantastic. The police come and arrest Mr and Mrs Grunge. Then they dig up their backyard. They find lots of jewellery and watches and video recorders. 'We have been looking for these thieves for a long time,' says the police chief. 'There is a big reward. Two thousand dollars.'

40

Yes, TWO THOUSAND.

So I get the reward. And the fifty dollars as well. And my picture is in the paper and I am on television. Dad and Brook and Mum are so proud of me.

And just to top it all off, I never wet the bed again.

Yes, NEVER.

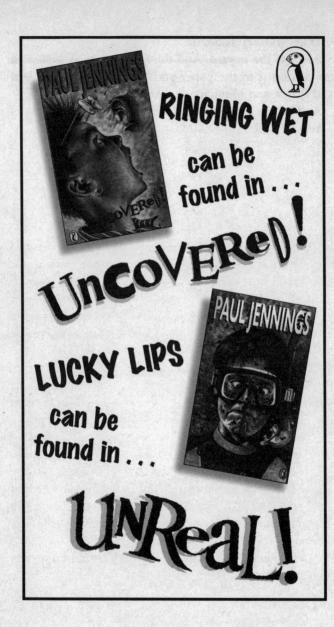

LUCKY LIPS

Marcus felt silly. He was embarrassed. But he knocked on the door anyway. There was no answer from inside the dark house. It was as silent as the grave. Then he noticed a movement behind the curtain; someone was watching him. He could see a dark eye peering through a chink in the curtain. There was a rustling noise inside that sounded like rats' feet on a bare floor.

The door slowly opened and Ma Scritchet's face appeared. It was true what people said – she looked like a witch. She had hair like straw and her nose was hooked and long. She smiled showing pointed, yellow teeth.

'Come in,' she said. 'I have been waiting for you.'

Marcus was not going to let this old woman fool him. 'How could you be expecting me?' he answered. 'No one knew I was coming here.' He felt better now. He could see that it was all a trick. She was a faker. A phoney. Did she really expect him to believe that she knew he was coming?

'I knew you were coming,' she said. 'And I know *why* you have come.'

This time Marcus knew she was lying. He had not told anyone about his problem. There was not one person in the world that knew about it, it was too embarrassing. The other kids would laugh if they knew.

He decided to go home. But first he would stir this old bag up a bit. 'Okay, Ma,' he said. 'Why have I come?'

She looked him straight in the eye. 'You are sixteen years old,' she told him. 'And you have never been kissed.'

Marcus could feel his face turning red. He was blushing. She knew – she knew all about it. She must be able to read minds. The stories that were told about her must be true. He felt silly and small, and he didn't know what to do.

Ma Scritchet started to laugh, a long cackling laugh. It made Marcus shiver. 'Come with me,' she said. She led him along a dark, narrow passage and up some wooden stairs. The house was filled with junk: broken TV sets and old bicycles, piles of books and empty bottles. The stair rails were covered in cobwebs. They went into a small room at the top of the house.

Inside the room was a couch and a chair. Nothing else. It was not what Marcus had expected. He thought there would be a crystal ball on a round table and lots of junk and equipment for telling fortunes. The room was almost bare.

2

Ma Scritchet held out her hand. 'This will cost you twenty dollars,' she said to Marcus.

'I pay after, not before,' said Marcus. 'This could be a trick.'

'You pay before, not after,' said Ma Scritchet. 'I only help those that believe in me.' Marcus looked into her eyes. They were cold and hard. He took out his wallet and gave her twenty dollars, and she tucked it inside her dress. Then she said, 'Lie down on the couch.'

Marcus lay on the couch and stared at the ceiling. A tiny spider was spinning a web in the corner. Marcus felt foolish lying there on a couch in this old woman's house. He wished he hadn't come; he wanted to go home. But there was something about Ma Scritchet that made him nervous. And now that he had paid his twenty dollars he was going to get his money's worth. 'Well,' he said. 'I suppose that you want me to tell you about my problem.'

'No,' said Ma Scritchet. 'I will tell you about it. You just stay there and listen.' Marcus did as she said.

'You have never kissed a girl,' said the old woman in a low voice. 'You have tried plenty of times. But they always turn you down. They think you are stuck up and selfish. They don't like the things you say about other people. Some girls go out with you once, but when you get home to their front door they always say, "Thank you" and go inside.'

Marcus listened in silence. Most of it was true. He knew he wasn't stuck up and selfish, but the rest of it was right. He tried everything he could think of. He would take a girl to the movies and buy her chocolates. He would even pay for her to get in. But then, right at the end when they were saying 'good night', he would close his eyes, pucker up his lips and lean forward, to find himself kissing the closed front door of the girl's house. It was maddening. It was enough to make him spit. And it had happened dozens of times. Not one girl would give him a kiss.

3

'Well,' said Marcus to Ma Scritchet. 'Can you help me? That's what I gave you the twenty dollars for.'

She smiled but said nothing. It was not a nice smile. It was a smile that made Marcus feel foolish. She stood up without a word and left the room, and Marcus could hear her footsteps clipping down the stairs. A minute or so later. he heard her coming back. She came into the room and held out a small tube. 'Take this,' she said. 'It's just what you need. This will do the trick.'

Marcus took it out of her hand and looked at it. It was a stick of lipstick in a small gold container. 'I'm not wearing lipstick,' Marcus told her. 'You must think I'm crazy.' He sat up and jumped off the couch. This had gone far enough. He wondered if he could get his money back.

'Sit down, boy,' said Ma Scritchet in a cold voice. 'And listen to me. You put that on your lips and you will get all the kisses you want. It has no colour. It's clear and no one will be able to see it. But it will do the trick. It will work on any female. Just put some of that on your lips and the nearest girl will want to kiss you.'

Marcus looked at the tube of lipstick. He didn't know whether to believe it or not. It might work. Old Ma Scritchet could read his mind; she knew what his problem was without being told. This lipstick could be just what he needed. 'Okay,' he said. 'I'll give it a try. But it had better work. If it doesn't, I will be back for my twenty dollars.'

'It will work,' hissed Ma Scritchet. 'It will work better than you think. Now it's time for you to go. The session is over.' She led Marcus down the narrow stairs and along the passage to the front door. He stepped out into the sunlight. It was bright and made him blink. As Ma Scritchet closed the door she told Marcus one more thing. 'This lipstick will only work once on each person. One girl: one kiss. That's the way it works.'

She closed the door in his face without saying another thing. Once more the old house was quiet.

4

Marcus kept the lipstick for a week before he used it. When he got home to his room with his record player and the posters on the wall, the whole thing seemed like a dream. The old house and Ma Scritchet were from another world. He wondered whether or not the visit had really happened, but he had the lipstick to prove that it had.

He held it in his hand. It had a strange appearance and he found that it glowed in the dark. He put it in a drawer and left it there.

Later that week a new girl started at Marcus's school. Her name was Jill. Marcus didn't waste any time; he asked her out for a date on her first day at school. She didn't seem too keen about going with him, but she was shy and didn't want to seem unfriendly, especially as she didn't know anyone at the school. In the end she agreed to go to a disco with him on Friday night.

Marcus arranged to meet Jill inside the disco. That way he wouldn't have to pay for her to get in. It wasn't a bad turn and Jill seemed to enjoy it. As he danced

Marcus could feel the lipstick in his pocket. He couldn't forget about it; it annoyed him. It was like having a stone in his shoe.

At eleven o'clock they decided to go home. It was only a short walk back to Jill's house. As they walked, Jill chatted happily; she was glad that she had made a new friend so quickly. Marcus started to feel a bit guilty. He fingered the lipstick in his pocket. Should he use it? He remembered something about stolen kisses. Was he stealing a kiss if he used the lipstick? Not really – if it worked Jill would be kissing him of her own free will. Anyway, it probably wouldn't work. Old Ma Scritchet had probably played a trick on him. He would never know unless he tried it. He just had to know if the lipstick worked, and this was his big chance.

As they went inside the front gate of Jill's house, Marcus pretended to bend down and do up his shoelace. He quickly pulled out the lipstick and smeared some on his lips. Then he stood up. His lips were tingling. He noticed that Jill was looking at him in a strange way; her eyes were wide open and staring. Then she rushed forward, threw her arms around Marcus's neck and kissed him. Marcus was so surprised that he nearly fell over.

Jill jumped back as if she had been burned. She put her hand up to her mouth and went red in the face. 'I, I, I'm sorry, Marcus. I don't know what came over me. What must you think of me? I've never done anything like that before.'

'Don't worry about it. That sort of thing happens to me all the time. The girls find me irresistible.'

Jill didn't know what to say. She was blushing. She couldn't understand what had happened. 'I'd better go in,' she said. 'I'm really sorry. I didn't mean to do that.' Then she turned around and rushed into the house.

Marcus whistled to himself as he walked home. 'It works,' he thought. 'The lipstick really works.' He couldn't wait to try it on someone else.

5

It was not so easy for Marcus to find his next victim. None of the girls at school wanted to go out with him. It was no use asking Jill again, as the lipstick only worked once on each person. He asked ten girls to go to the pictures with him and they all said 'no'.

He started to get cross. 'Stuck up snobs,' he said to himself. 'I'll teach them a lesson.' He decided to make the most popular girl in the school kiss him. That would show them all. Her name was Fay Billings.

The trouble was that he knew she wouldn't go out on a date with him. Then he had a bright idea: he wouldn't even bother about a date. He would just go around to Fay's house and ask to see her. He would put the lipstick on before he arrived, and when she came to the door she would give him a big kiss. The news would soon get around and the other kids would think he had something good going. It would make him popular with the girls.

Marcus grinned. It was a great idea. He decided to put it into action straight away. He rode his bike around to Fay's house and leaned it against the fence. Then he took out the lipstick and put some on his lips. He walked up to the front door and rang the bell with a big smile on his face.

No one answered the door. He could hear a vacuum cleaner going inside so he rang the bell again. The sound of the vacuum cleaner stopped and Mrs Billings appeared at the door. She was about forty. She had a towel wrapped around her head and had dust on her face from the housework she had been doing. She had never seen Marcus before; he was not one of Fay's friends.

Mrs Billings was just going to ask Marcus what he wanted when a strange look came over her face. Her eyes went large and round. They looked as if they were going to pop out. Then she threw her arms around Marcus's neck and kissed him on the mouth.

It was hard to say who was more surprised, Marcus or Mrs Billings. They sprang apart and looked around to see if anyone had seen what happened. Marcus didn't want anyone to see him being kissed by a forty-year-old woman. How embarrassing. 'My goodness,' said Mrs Billings. 'What am I doing? Kissing a perfect stranger. And you're so young. What has got into me? What would my husband think? Please excuse me. I must be ill. I think I had better go and have a little rest.' She turned around and walked slowly into the house. She shook her head as she went.

6

Marcus rode home slowly. He was not pleased. This was not working out the way he wanted. What if someone had seen him being kissed by an old lady like Mrs Billings? He would never live it down. He had had the lipstick for two weeks now and had only received one decent kiss. None of the girls would go out with him. And he couldn't wear the lipstick just anywhere – he didn't want any other mothers kissing him.

He decided to make Fay Billings kiss him at school, in front of all the other kids. That would show them that he had something special. All the girls would be chasing him after that; He would be the most popular boy in the school.

He picked his moment carefully. He sat next to Fay for the Maths lesson the next day. She looked at him with a funny expression on her face but she didn't say anything. Miss White was late for the class. She was a young teacher and was popular with the students, but she was always late. This was the chance that Marcus had been waiting for. He bent down under the desk and put on some of the lipstick. Then he sat up in the desk and looked at Fay.

The lipstick worked. Fay's eyes went round and she threw herself onto Marcus and kissed him. Then she jumped back and gave a little cry. Marcus looked around with a grin on his face, but it did not last for long. All the girls' eyes were wide and staring. Tissy came up and kissed him. And then Gerda and Helen and Betty and Maria. They climbed over each other in the rush to get to him. They shrieked and screamed and fought; they scratched and fought and bit. Marcus fell onto the floor under a struggling, squirming heap of girls.

When all the sixteen girls in the class had kissed him there was silence. They were in a state of shock – they couldn't understand what had happened. They just sat there looking at each other. Marcus had his tie ripped off and his shirt was torn. He had a cut lip and a black eye.

Then Gerda yelled out, 'I kissed Marcus! Arrgghh . . .' She rushed over to the tap and started washing her mouth out. All the girls started wiping their mouths as if they had eaten something nasty. Then everybody started laughing. The boys laughed, and the girls laughed. They rolled around the floor holding their sides. Tears rolled out of their eyes. Everybody laughed, except Marcus.

He knew that they were laughing at him. And he didn't think that it was funny.

7

After all the kissing at school everyone called Marcus 'Lucky Lips'. Nobody liked Marcus any better than before and the girls still stayed away from him. Everyone talked about the kissing session for a while; then they forgot about it and talked about other things. But Marcus didn't forget about it. He felt like a fool. Everyone had laughed at him. He was worse off now than he had been before.

He thought about taking the lipstick back to Ma Scritchet and telling her what he thought about it, but he was too scared. There was something creepy about that old lady and he didn't really want to see her again.

Marcus didn't use the lipstick again for about a month. None of the girls would go out with him and he wasn't going to risk wearing it just anywhere. Not after what happened at school that day. But he always carried the lipstick with him, just in case.

The last time he used it was at the Royal Melbourne Show. The whole class at school went there on an excursion. They had to collect material for an assignment. Marcus and Fay Billings and two other boys walked around together. The others didn't really want Marcus with them; they thought he was a show off. But they let him tag along. They didn't want to hurt his feelings.

The favourite spots at the show were the sideshows. There were knock-em-downs and rides on the Mad Mouse. There was a fat lady and a mirror maze. There was a ghost train and dozens of other rides. One of the side shows had a sign up saying 'BIG BEN THE STRONGEST MAN IN THE WORLD'.

They all milled around looking at the tent. It was close to one of the animal pavilions. There was a great hall full of pigs nearby. 'Let's go and look at the pigs,' said Fay.

'No,' answered Marcus. 'Who wants to look at filthy pigs. Let's go and see Big Ben. He fights people. Anyone who can beat him wins one thousand dollars and gets to kiss the Queen Of The Show.'

'That would be just the thing for Lucky Lips,' said Fay. They all laughed, except Marcus. He went red in the face.

'I could get a kiss from the Queen Of The Show,' he said. They all laughed again. 'All right,' said Marcus. 'Just watch me.' He paid his dollar and went inside Big Ben's tent. The others all followed him; they wanted to see what was going to happen.

Inside the tent was a boxing ring. Big Ben was standing inside it waiting for someone to fight him and try to win the thousand dollars and a kiss from the Queen Of The Show. She sat on a high chair behind the ring. Marcus looked at her. She was beautiful; he wouldn't mind a kiss from her. Then he looked at Big Ben. He was the biggest man Marcus had ever seen. He had huge muscles and was covered in tattoos. And he looked mean – very mean.

Marcus ducked around the ring to where the Queen Of The Show sat. He quickly put on some of the invisible lipstick, and at once the beauty queen jumped off her chair and kissed Marcus. Everyone laughed except Big Ben. He roared in fury. 'Trying to steal a kiss without a fight, are you?' he yelled. 'I'll teach you a lesson, my boy.'

Marcus tried to run away but he was not quick enough. Big Ben grabbed him and lifted Marcus high into the air. Then he walked outside the tent and across to the pig pavilion. Marcus wriggled and yelled, but it was no good; he couldn't get away. Big Ben carried Marcus over to one of the pig pens and threw him inside.

Marcus crashed to the floor of the pen. He felt dizzy. The world seemed to be spinning around. He tried to stand up, but he couldn't. The floor was covered in foul smelling muck. In the corner Marcus could see the biggest pig that he had ever seen. It was eating rotten vegetables and slops from a trough. It was dribbling and slobbering as it ate. Its teeth were green. It turned around and looked at Marcus. It was a sow.

Marcus suddenly remembered something that Ma Scritchet had said about the lipstick. She had said: 'It will work on any female.' Marcus started to scream. 'Get me out. Get me out.'

But it was too late. The sow came over for her kiss.

10 Unbelievable! Things About
PAUL JENNINGS

1. It's Unbelievable! He would love to visit another planet!

2. If he hadn't become a writer Paul would have loved to have been a musician. He plays the melodeon (button accordion).

3. Paul is crazy about classic cars and races them at weekends.

4. His favourite car is an MG.

5. The most thrilling moment of his life was getting UnReal! published.

6. Paul loves the smell of gum trees and sea mist.

7. His favourite music is sixties rock, folk music and Chopin.

8. It's almost Unmentionable! but when he was 12 Paul put a dead rat in the fridge. (His mother was unimpressed!)

9. Burgundy is Paul's favourite colour.

10. Unsurprisingly, Paul's nickname is Jens!

PAUL JENNINGS *Unmasked!*

Paul Jennings was born in England in 1943 and moved to Australia when he was 6 years old. He now lives near Melbourne with his wife Claire and their family.

Paul spends most of his time writing his books in a small oak panelled attic room with lead-light windows overlooking the mountain valleys of Melbourne. When he plans a story he jots down his ideas in a special book as soon as they come into his head. A lot of the stories stem either from his own childhood, when he was always embarrassed by something or other, or from a funny story or something he's seen. Paul never starts writing until he has the whole story worked out in his head. Then he writes an outline in his old exercise book and finally types the story out on his word processor and sends it off to his publisher.

- ✂ - - - - - - -

PAUL JENNINGS

HE'S
UNstoPPabLE!

Dear Bookseller,

Return this voucher before 28 February 1998 to: PAUL JENNINGS OFFER, CHILDREN'S MARKETING DEPT., PUFFIN BOOKS, 27 WRIGHTS LANE, LONDON W8 5TZ

Puffin Books will ensure, on presentation of this voucher, that you are refunded, or your account will be credited (if you have an account with us), 65p for one Paul Jennings Puffin Book sold before 31 January 1998.

To be completed by bookseller:

BOOKSHOP WHERE REDEEMED _____

ADDRESS _____

_____

POSTCODE _____ **DATE** _____

PENGUIN ACCOUNT NUMBER (if known) _____

Cash value 0.0001p